Smart Sarah
and the Magic of Science

A Technology Expresso Publications
www.technologyexpresso.com

3475 Oak Valley Road Suite 650
Atlanta, Georgia 30326

ISBN: 978-1-4834-8498-3 (sc)
ISBN: 978-1-4834-8499-0 (e)

Lulu Publishing Services rev. date: 05/15/2018

Smart Sarah

and the Magic of Science

by Jacqueline Sanders-Blackman

Meet the Maker Family

Once upon a time there was a little girl named Smart Sarah, who loved colorful things.

Her bedroom was filled with colorful things. One day Smart Sarah asked her Mother a question that she remembers to this day, "How are colors made?"

Her Mother chuckled and said, "Colors are made in so many ways. Just keep your eyes open and you will learn."

Smart Sarah was okay with her Mother's answer for a while but as Smart Sarah began to grow older the question never went away. She was always very curious about how colors were made.

Well, Smart Sarah's curiosity really came out right when she was about to turn 8. It was about 10 days before her birthday when she was helping her big brother paint a big red "M" on his bedroom wall to match the school colors at his college. Smart Sarah said to her big brother, "I always wondered how colors are made."

Smart Sarah's big brother, Talented Terrance told her confidently, "Color is made from pigment." Smart Sarah thought, now we are getting somewhere. *Pigment*, she thought. *That's an important word.* She was okay with the answer from her big brother for now.

Then one day when her grandfather was picking her up from the bus stop, as they were walking home, her grandfather said, "Look, in the sky." Smart Sarah looked up and there was a rainbow. She remembered the important word *pigment*. She said to her grandfather, "That rainbow has a lot of pigment."

Her grandfather laughed and said, "Pigment – that's a very smart and important word! Did you learn that at school?" "Nope," she said, referring to Talented Terrance. "Big brother told me color is made from pigment." Her grandfather agreed, "Yes, indeed it does."

Grandfather said to Smart Sarah, "Did you know nature has its own special formula for creating color without using pigment?"

She said, "It does?" with excitement!

She was sure her wise grandfather knew lots of secrets and formulas about nature, and she was old enough to learn about one of them today.

"When the Sun is shining and it is raining at the same time, the rain passes through the Sunlight, and rain actually bends the white light. The rays given off by the Sun create the colors of the rainbow," said grandfather. "WOW! It bends the rays of the Sun?" she exclaimed. All the way home Smart Sarah could only say WOW!

Saturday morning came and Smart Sarah's dad and brother PJ were washing the car. Smart Sarah headed outside to help him wash the car.

She asked her dad, "Do you know that when water and sunlight come together, a rainbow appears?" Her dad responded, "Oh, really?"

Then, he started looking at the sky until he found what he was looking for, the Sun. He then pointed the garden hose in the air.

Smart Sarah started to giggle as droplets of water fell on her from dad's towering hands holding the garden hose so high. As Smart Sarah and her brother PJ looked up, she saw her daddy was simulating the raindrops, and as the sunlight hit the drops of water, the water drops turned red, orange, yellow, green blue and purple.

After helping her dad wash the car, a soggy Smart Sarah made her way into the house. Her mother was in the kitchen stirring and mixing up what was surely a batter for some cupcakes. Smart Sarah was so excited to tell her mom, "Daddy made me a rainbow." Her mom replied, "Oh he did?"

"Yes, he did," Smart Sarah replied. "He made some raindrops with the water hose and waved them in front of the sun. The water drops bent the sun's rays into 7 different colors to make the rainbow."

Her mom was tickled and just continued to chuckle while still stirring the frosting for the cupcakes.

Smart Sarah sampled the cupcake frosting from outside of the mixing bowl, just as her mother asked, "Speaking of colors, what color icing should I make?" "Well," Smart Sarah said, sounding a little disappointed, "You only have three colors: yellow, red and blue. So I guess one of those will have to do."

Her mother looked at her from a side glance. "I can actually make any color; all I have to do is mix together one or two of the colors," she said. Smart Sarah said, "You never told me you could make colors!"

Her mom replied, "Well watch this. I can take blue and yellow and mix them together and they become green. I can mix red and yellow and now we have orange." Smart Sarah was jumping around and doing cartwheels with excitement after tasting the blended sugar-filled and colorful cupcake frosting that came from her mother's demonstrations.

When Smart Sarah made her way from the kitchen to the bathroom, there was no surprise big sister Nurturing Nola was in the mirror doing her makeup. With excitement Smart Sarah said, "Guess what Nola? Mom invented new colors in the kitchen." Nola saw all the smudges and smears on Smart Sarah's clothes and knew exactly what had occurred in the kitchen.

Smart Sarah hopped up on a stool and watched her sister apply her makeup. Big Sister said, "You're in my light. My makeup won't be right if you're in my light." Smart Sarah asked, "Why do you put on makeup?" Without a second thought Nola said, "It enhances my features. Some colors compliment and highlight my brown skin and other hues create contrast."

Smart Sarah paused a moment, then proudly she said, "I know what makes the colors you put on your face, it's called pigment." "Exactly, I'm very impressed, Little Sister. Some pigments you can buy from the store and some pigment we are born and blessed with. Our skin has a type of pigment called melanin, and that's what determines our skin, eye and hair color," Nola replied.

Smart Sarah has endless curiosity. Always more questions, she asked, "Nola, so why do you think we have to buy stuff to make our hair purple? Why are people not born with purple hair?" With a sigh, Big Sis said, "Go away, go away baby sister, that's enough questions for one day."

The time had flown by; it was almost Smart Sarah's 8th birthday. The family came together to decide what to do for Smart Sarah's special day. She was so curious and especially curious about colors. That's the one thing they all could agree on.

Grandfather suggested, "Let's get her a dress with all the colors of the rainbow?" Mom said, "Let's get her an easy bake oven?" Big sister said, "How about getting her purple hair extensions?" Everyone paused and gave her the side eye. Then Big Brother said, "How about a paint set?" Dad said, "How about those machines that create bubbles?" Mom said, "How about a dress with lots of color and bows?"

Everyone liked their own ideas and so they just couldn't agree. Then Grandmother spoke up, "I got the perfect gift idea…" "What is it?" they asked in unison. "Never you mind," she replied.

So on the Big Day Smart Sarah cried out, "Grand Mommy, I love it!"

Grandmommy had given Smart Sarah a super size Science kit with 101 experiments, complete with a lab coat, gloves, test tubes and goggles. Smart Sarah could mix, create, blend and bend light using her imagination and curiosity.

Smart Sarah from that day forward would tell anyone how much she loved Science. "Because science you see is better than magic...it's magic that is nature-made that helps enhance our lives everyday!"

When Smart Sarah grows up, her curiosity and love for science could lead her into so many directions and careers;

- ★ Medicine
- ★ Biologist
- ★ Chemist
- ★ Food Science
- ★ Forensics
- ★ Geography
- ★ Marine Biologist
- ★ Meteorologist
- ★ Microbiologist
- ★ Pharmacist
- ★ Plant Scientist
- ★ Veterinarian
- ★ Wildlife Biologist
- ★ Zoologist

Do
you
Know
a

Future
Science SUPERSTAR?

It Might Be the Person You See In Your Mirror Everyday

This is the End of the Story
but let it be the
start of your
family fun with science
home projects!

STEAM Activity Guide

Exploring Science and Environment

1. Homemade Soap, https://www.education.com/activity/article/Make_Soap_middle/
2. Predict the Weather, https://www.education.com/activity/article/Weather_Forecaster_middle/
3. Experiment with Magnet Magic, https://www.education.com/activity/article/Magnet_Magic_middle/
4. Stored Energy, https://www.education.com/activity/article/Returning_Rod_middle/
5. Disappearing Crystals: A Refraction Experiment, https://www.education.com/activity/article/Disappearing_Crystals_middle/
6. Find a Flower, https://www.education.com/activity/article/Flower_Spy_middle/
7. Experiment with Magnetism: Make a Hanging Compass, https://www.education.com/activity/article/hanging-compass/
8. Clean Water Using the Sun, https://www.education.com/activity/article/Cleaning_Water_middle/

9. Spin the Bucket: A Centripetal Force Experiment, https://www.education.com/activity/article/Centripetal_Force_middle/
10. Can Crusher Experiment, https://www.education.com/activity/article/Crunch_Can_middle/
11. Grow Your Own Herbs, https://www.education.com/activity/article/Historic_Herb_Garden/
12. Landscape Photography, https://www.education.com/activity/article/landscape-photography/
13. Make a Molecule, https://www.education.com/activity/article/clay-molecule-model/
14. How Do Oil Spills Harm Wildlife?, https://www.education.com/activity/article/oil-spills-harm-wildlife/
15. How to Make an Ethernet Cable, https://www.education.com/activity/article/assemble-ethernet-cable/
16. Be a Botanist: Make Herbarium Sheets, https://www.education.com/activity/article/Herbarium_Sheets/
17. Experiment with Salt Water Conductivity, https://www.education.com/activity/article/Experiment_with_Salt_Water/
18. Bread Mold Experiment, https://www.education.com/activity/article/Making_Mold_Science_Experiment/
19. Potato Cannon, https://www.education.com/activity/article/potato-cannon/
20. Extract DNA from Spinach!, https://www.education.com/activity/article/pull-dna-spinach/

For more information about the
STEAM Makers Series email:
Info@TechnologyeXpresso.com